Dear Parent:

Congratulations! Your child is taking the first steps on an exciting journey. The destination? Independent reading!

STEP INTO READING® will help your child get there. The program offers five steps to reading success. Each step includes fun stories and colorful art. There are also Step into Reading Sticker Books, Step into Reading Math Readers, Step into Reading Phonics Readers, Step into Reading Write-In Readers, and Step into Reading Phonics Boxed Sets—a complete literacy program with something to interest every child.

Learning to Read, Step by Step!

Ready to Read   Preschool–Kindergarten
• big type and easy words • rhyme and rhythm • picture clues
For children who know the alphabet and are eager to begin reading.

Reading with Help   Preschool–Grade 1
• basic vocabulary • short sentences • simple stories
For children who recognize familiar words and sound out new words with help.

Reading on Your Own   Grades 1–3
• engaging characters • easy-to-follow plots • popular topics
For children who are ready to read on their own.

Reading Paragraphs   Grades 2–3
• challenging vocabulary • short paragraphs • exciting stories
For newly independent readers who read simple sentences with confidence.

Ready for Chapters   Grades 2–4
• chapters • longer paragraphs • full-color art
For children who want to take the plunge into chapter books but still like colorful pictures.

STEP INTO READING® is designed to give every child a successful reading experience. The grade levels are only guides. Children can progress through the steps at their own speed, developing confidence in their reading, no matter what their grade.

Remember, a lifetime love of reading starts with a single step!

Special thanks to Sarah Buzby, Cindy Ledermann, Ann McNeill, Dana Koplik, Emily Kelly, Sharon Woloszyk, Tanya Mann, Julia Phelps, Rita Lichtwardt, Kathy Berry, Rob Hudnut, David Wiebe, Shelley Dvi-Vardhana, Michelle Cogan, Gabrielle Miles, Rainmaker Entertainment, and Walter P. Martishius

Visit us on the Web!
StepIntoReading.com
randomhouse.com/kids
www.barbie.com

Educators and librarians, for a variety of teaching tools, visit us at RHTeachersLibrarians.com

ISBN: 978-0-307-93196-2 (trade) — ISBN: 978-0-375-97113-6 (lib. bdg.)

Printed in the United States of America   11 10

Barbie
THE Princess & THE Popstar

STAR Power

Adapted by Mary Man-Kong

Based on the original screenplay by
Steve Granat and Cydne Clark

Illustrated by Ulkutay Design Group

Random House 🏠 New York

Tori is a princess.

She lives in a castle.

She wears fancy dresses
every day.

She wants
to try something new.
Tori wants
to be a pop star.

Keira is a pop star.
She works hard
all the time.
She is too busy
to have fun.

Keira wants

to be a princess.

Keira and Tori meet at the palace.

They become
good friends.

Tori has
a magical hairbrush.
It makes
glittering hairstyles.

Keira has
a magical microphone.
It makes
sparkling clothes.

Tori and Keira
use their gadgets
to look like each other!
They switch places.

Tori shows Keira
the royal secret garden.
Fairies protect
a diamond plant.
It gives the kingdom life.

The fairies give
Keira and Tori
diamond necklaces.

Keira and Tori
will be
best friends forever!

Tori teaches Keira
how to be a princess.

Keira teaches Tori

how to be a pop star.

Tori sings and dances
in the spotlight.
She has
a perfect pop star day!

Keira dresses up and
rides in a carriage.
She has
a perfect princess day!

The next day,
Tori trips.
It is hard work
being a pop star.

Keira does not act
like a princess.
It is hard work
being a princess.

Keira has a pillow fight
with Tori's sisters.

They laugh.

They jump and play.

Keira has lots of fun.

She writes a happy song.

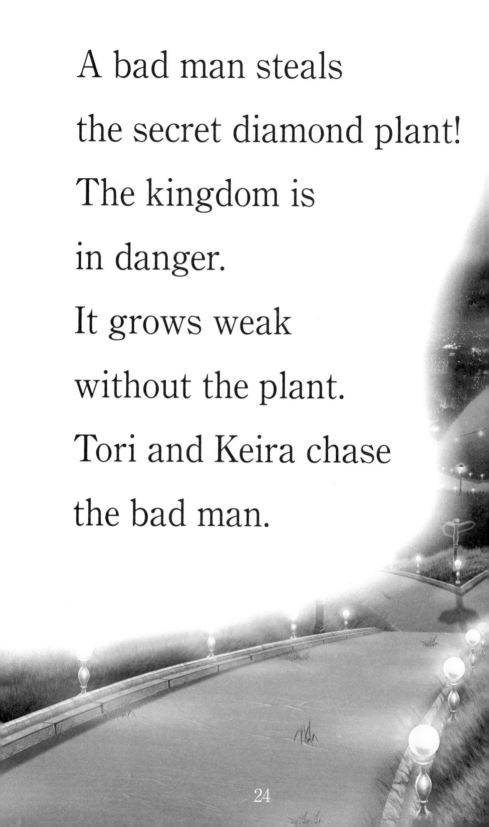

A bad man steals
the secret diamond plant!
The kingdom is
in danger.
It grows weak
without the plant.
Tori and Keira chase
the bad man.

Tori and Keira get the
diamond plant back.
They put it
in the ground.

The diamond plant
will not grow.

The kingdom is doomed!

The girls remember
their necklaces!
They plant the diamonds
from the necklaces.

Two new plants bloom.

The kingdom is saved!

Tori learns she likes
being a princess best.
She promises to care
for her kingdom.

Keira learns she likes
being a pop star best.
She has a new song
for her fans.

Keira and Tori
sing together
at Keira's concert.
The girls rock!